W9-AGT-250

Hello, Family Members,

Learning to read is one of the most important accomplishments of early childhood. **Hello Reader!** books are designed to help children become skilled readers who like to read. Beginning readers learn to read by remembering frequently used words like "the," "is," and "and"; by using phonics skills to decode new words; and by interpreting picture and text clues. These books provide both the stories children enjoy and the structure they need to read fluently and independently. Here are suggestions for helping your child *before*, *during*, and *after* reading:

Before

- Look at the cover and pictures and have your child predict what the story is about.
- Read the story to your child.
- Encourage your child to chime in with familiar words and phrases.
- Echo read with your child by reading a line first and having your child read it after you do.

During

- Have your child think about a word he or she does not recognize right away. Provide hints such as "Let's see if we know the sounds" and "Have we read other words like this one?"
- Encourage your child to use phonics skills to sound out new words.
- Provide the word for your child when more assistance is needed so that he or she does not struggle and the experience of reading with you is a positive one.
- Encourage your child to have fun by reading with a lot of expression . . . like an actor!

After

- Have your child keep lists of interesting and favorite words.
- Encourage your child to read the books over and over again. Have him or her read to brothers, sisters, grandparents, and even teddy bears. Repeated readings develop confidence in young readers.
- Talk about the stories. Ask and answer questions. Share ideas about the funniest and most interesting characters and events in the stories.

I do hope that you and your child enjoy this book.

　　　　　—Francie Alexander
　　　　　Reading Specialist,
　　　　　Scholastic's Learning Ventures

For my sister Susan,
craftswoman extraordinaire!
— J.M.

Special thanks to Bill Hoffman for craft page computer graphics
Cut-paper photography by Paul Dyer

Copyright © 2000 by Judith Moffatt.
All rights reserved. Published by Scholastic Inc.
SCHOLASTIC, HELLO READER, CARTWHEEL BOOKS and associated logos
are trademarks and/or registered trademarks of Scholastic Inc.

Library of Congress Cataloging-in-Publication Data
Moffatt, Judith.
    Bugs : a read-and-do book / by Judith Moffatt.
       p.   cm. — (Hello reader! Level 2)
    Summary: Minky and his friend Mouse provide instructions and helpful hints for making paper bugs.
    ISBN 0-439-09859-9
    1. Paper work—Juvenile literature. 2. Insects in art—Juvenile literature. [1. Paper work. 2. Handicraft. 3. Insects in art.] I. Title. II. Series.
TT870.M529   2000
736'.98—dc21
                                                                99-28967
                                                                    CIP
12 11 10 9 8 7 6 5 4 3 2 1   00 01 02 03 04

Printed in the U.S.A.   24
First printing, September 2000

BUGS
A READ-AND-DO BOOK
by Judith Moffatt

Hello Reader! —Level 2

SCHOLASTIC INC.

New York   Toronto   London   Auckland   Sydney
Mexico City   New Delhi   Hong Kong

Hi! My name is Minky.
This is my friend Mouse.

We're here to help you make
paper bugs for your house.

Gather up your scissors, pencil, hole punch, tape, and glue.

Find lots of colored
papers—red, black,
purple, green, and blue.

A caterpillar snacks
on leaves until it
changes shape.

CATERPILLAR

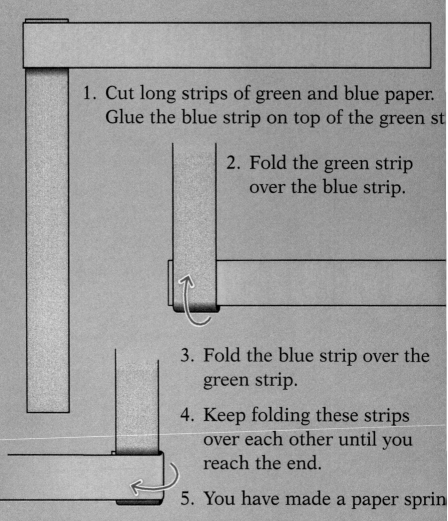

1. Cut long strips of green and blue paper. Glue the blue strip on top of the green st

2. Fold the green strip over the blue strip.

3. Fold the blue strip over the green strip.

4. Keep folding these strips over each other until you reach the end.

5. You have made a paper sprin

6. Make another spring and tape it to the end of this one.

7. Glue on a face with eyes, antennae, and a mouth.

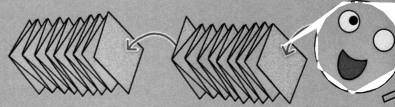

You can make it
longer by adding parts
with tape.

This bug has made
a magic change into
a butterfly.

BUTTERFL...

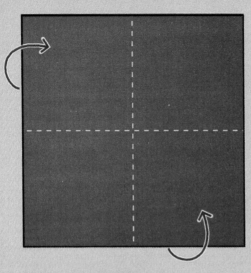

1. Fold a square piec
   of paper in half.

2. Fold it in half
   again to make a
   small square.

3. Round off three of the square
   edges with your scissors.
   Be careful not to cut the
   folded corner.

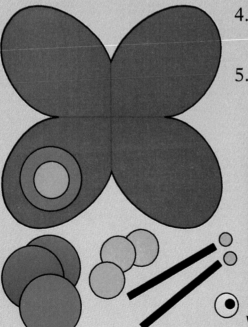

4. Unfold. Now you hav
   the butterfly's wings!

5. Add a thick strip for
   the body.

6. Add eyes,
   antennae,
   and a mouth.
   Decorate the
   wings.

7. Hole punch th
   top so you can
   hang it.

Hang him where
there is a breeze
so he can flutter by.

A ladybug is black and red.
She hides her flying wings.

LADYBUG

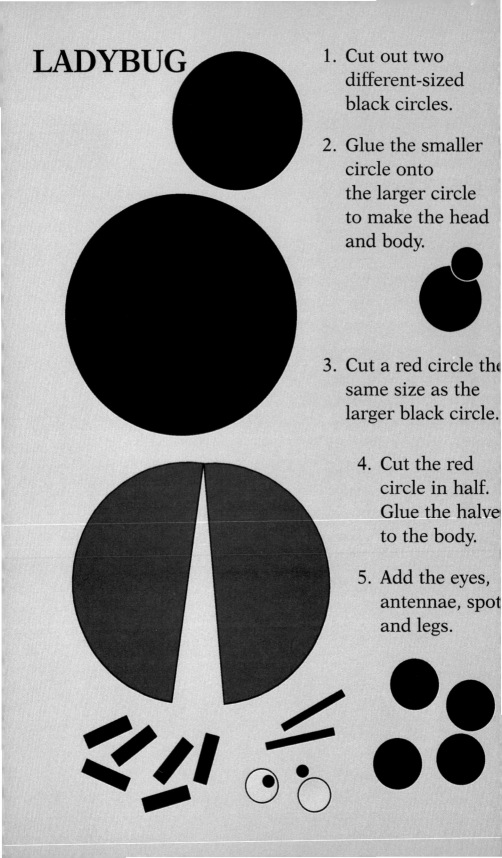

1. Cut out two different-sized black circles.

2. Glue the smaller circle onto the larger circle to make the head and body.

3. Cut a red circle the same size as the larger black circle.

4. Cut the red circle in half. Glue the halves to the body.

5. Add the eyes, antennae, spots and legs.

Everybody loves her—just
see what luck she brings!

The fastest bug is the dragonfly, who zooms with a buzzing sound.

DRAGONFLY

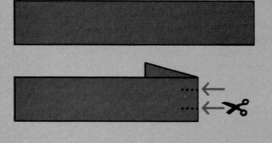

1. Cut a long strip of paper for the body

2. Fold the body and cut two small slits as shown. Unfold.

3. Cut a sheet of pap in half for the win

4. Fold the paper back and forth so it looks like a small fan.

5. Push the wing through the slits.
   Hole punch the bottom so you can hang it.

6. Add eyes and decorate the body.

With his great big eyes,
he sees very well—
make them large
and round.

The spider with eight tiny leg
builds a web in just an hour.

SPIDER

1. Cut out two different-sized paper circles.

2. Glue the smaller circle onto the larger circle to make the head and body.

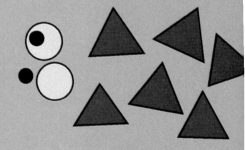

3. Add eyes and decorate the spider's back.

4. Cut eight thin strips of paper for the legs.

5. Fold each leg twice as shown. Add triangle feet to the short folded ends.

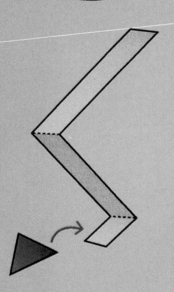

6. Glue the eight finished legs underneath your spider's body.

Tape her to your window,
and she'll give you
spider power.

Now your room is full of bugs
You've brought the outside in!

hink of new bugs you can
1ake, and start all over again.

HELPFUL HINTS
from Minky and Mouse

1. To make round circles—find different-sized coins, cans, and jar lids. Trace the round shapes onto the back side of your paper with a pencil. Take your time to cut carefully.

2. Use small amounts of glue. The paper won't wrinkle as much, and your bugs will dry faster.